The Crimson Ribbon

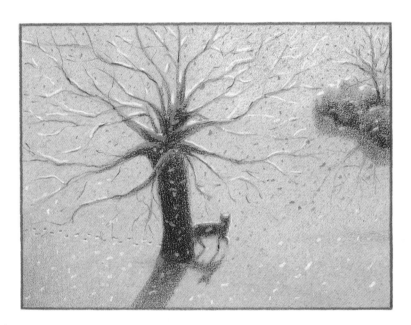

HILARY HORDER HIPPELY

ILLUSTRATED BY

JO ELLEN McALLISTER STAMMEN

G. P. PUTNAM'S SONS · NEW YORK

JE

G. P. Putnam's Sons, a division of The Putnam & Grosset Group, 200 Madison Avenue, New York, NY 10016.
G. P. Putnam's Sons, Reg. U.S. Pat. & Tm. Off. Published simultaneously in Canada. Printed in Hong Kong by South China
Printing Co. (1988) Ltd. Book designed by Gunta Alexander. Text set in Kennerley.

Library of Congress Cataloging-in-Publication Data
Hippely, Hilary Horder.   The crimson ribbon / by Hilary Horder Hippely; illustrated by Joellen McAllister-Stammen.   p.
cm.   Summary: Nell wishes she had nice, old aunts like her mother had and, for one brief afternoon, she does. [1. Great-
aunts—Fiction.] I. McAllister, Jo Ellen Stammen, ill. II. Title.   PZ7.H5977Cr   1994   [E]—dc20   92-43066   CIP   AC

ISBN 0-399-22542-0
1   3   5   7   9   10   8   6   4   2

One gray November afternoon, Nell sat at the kitchen table, wishing she could think of something fun to do.

"Why don't you come on up to the attic with me?" Mom suggested.

"I need to put some things away, and you might have fun
poking through my old green trunk."

Nell sighed. "All right," she said, putting on her sweater and
trudging up the creaky back steps.

The trunk smelled of old clothes and spice.

Nell opened up a small box. "Look, Mom," she said, pulling out a handful of ribbons. "Were these yours when you were little?"

Mom nodded. "Aunt Olive and Aunt Frances gave me a ribbon whenever I went to visit. And they gave them special names. This one's azure, Nell, and here's violet and jonquil."

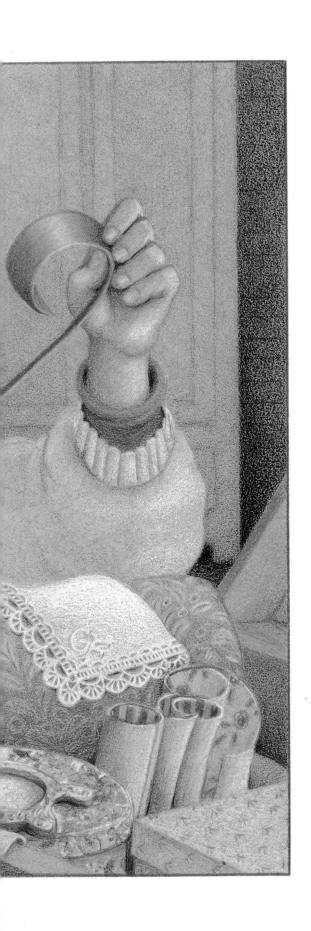

"What's this ribbon called?" Nell asked.

"That's crimson." Mom smiled. "You know, if I close my eyes I can see my aunts right now, combing my hair and telling me stories of when they were little."

Nell sighed. "I wish I had nice old aunts."

Mom kissed Nell's forehead. "I wish you did, too, because you're just the kind of girl they'd like." She stood up. "Now I'm going downstairs. Can you find something up here to do?"

Nell didn't answer. She was kneeling on the window seat
and staring outside. It had grown dark, and tiny flakes of snow
drifted past the streetlight.

"Look, Mom, it's snowing!" But her mother had already gone
downstairs.

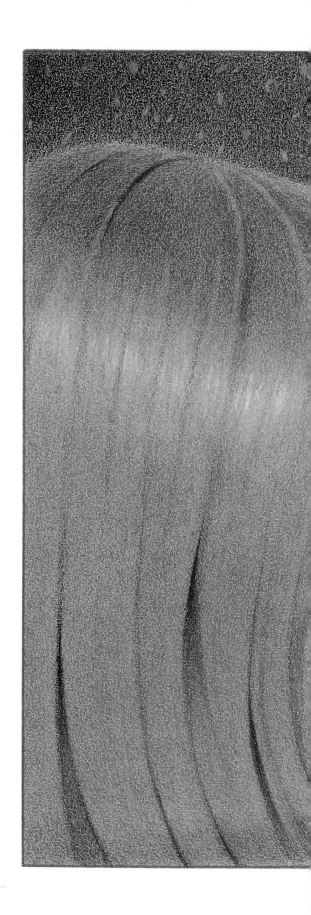

Nell leaned close to the icy pane. She watched flakes fall on the porch and roof and chimney of the little house across the street where nobody lived.

"You look nice all covered with snow," Nell told the little house. "I wish someone lived in you, someone old and cozy."

All at once a glimmer of light appeared in the window, and wisps of smoke twirled out the chimney. Nell pressed her nose against the pane.

Two old ladies were sitting in rocking chairs beside a fire.

Olive put down her knitting and stretched.

"Ho hum," she yawned. "Are you awake, Frances?"

"Yes, Olive," murmured her sister, straightening up and opening one eye. "I'm just trying to think of something fun to do. I wish Nell could visit."

"Me, too," said Olive. "But do you think Nell could come visiting on such a cold winter day?"

Just then there was a knock at the door. The two sisters clapped their hands.

"Hurrah!" cried Olive. "She's here!"

Frances smiled. "And just in time for tea!"

Nell took off her hat and coat and hung them by the fire. "I'll put on the kettle," she said.

The kitchen was warm and smelled of chocolate. Nell took a
tray off the wall and set it with cups and saucers and spoons,
and a flowered pot for tea. She found a tin labeled TREATS.

"How many cookies would you like?" she called.

"Five each," answered Olive. "And don't forget the
cinnamon toast!"

Outside, the snow kept falling, but inside it was warm and light and cozy.

"Here's your stool," Olive said. "Sit between us so we can both see you."

Frances sipped her tea. "You really are a treasure, Nell," she said. "We're so lucky you live across the street."

"I'm lucky, too," said Nell, settling a shawl over her knees. "Can you tell me about when you were little?"

"Let's see now." Frances smiled. "When we were your age we almost always wore dresses, even when we played. And we both had beautiful brown hair that shone in the firelight."

"Just like your hair," said Olive. "Only ours was long."

"All the way down our backs," added Frances. "It took forever to comb."

Nell reached for a cookie. "I wish I had long hair."

"Oh, no." Olive shook her head. "Your short hair looks lovely." She turned to Frances. "Perhaps Nell would like one of our nice, bright ribbons."

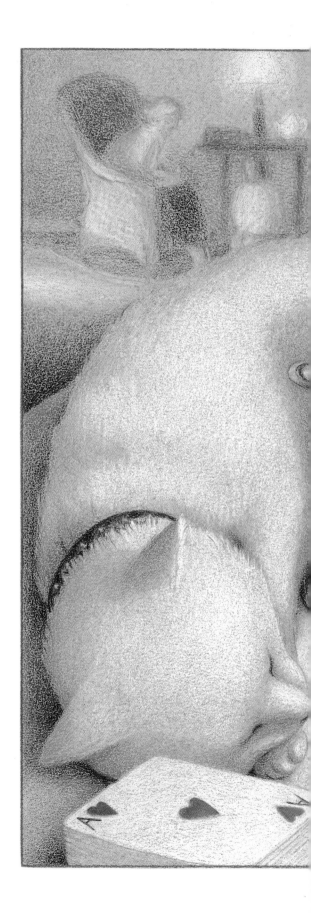

Frances reached for her sewing box. She pulled out a satin ribbon. "What do you think, Olive? Crimson seems just the color for Nell."

"Perfect," agreed Olive. "Crimson is full of imagination."

Nell ran the satin between her fingers. "It's beautiful."

"My ribbon is azure," said Frances, tying a blue ribbon in her hair. "Olive's ribbon has to be olive, but we like it anyway."

"Come hold the mirror, Nell," said Olive. "And I'll tie your bow."

Nell felt her hair being combed and the ribbon tied. She listened to the fire hiss as the logs burned low. Someone was calling her name.

In the kitchen her mother was setting soup bowls on a large white tray.

"There you are!" exclaimed Mom. "And don't you look nice. You've tied that red ribbon into a perfect bow."

Nell reached up to touch her hair. The ribbon felt soft and shiny and a little wet from the snow.

"It's a crimson ribbon," she reminded her mother. "Crimson is full of imagination."

Nell turned to look out the window. The little house looked back, almost winking under the starry sky.

"Goodnight, Olive," whispered Nell. "Goodnight, Frances."